Kalki The Arrival.

SriJoydip

SriJoydip

Dedication

Sun God

Book Name: **Kalki The Arrival**

All global publishing rights are held by

Sri Joydip Ashram

93 Itbhata Road, Burdwan -713103

http://srijoydipashram.wordpress.com

editor.subhadip@gmail.con

Published on 30th July 2025

4 Kalki The Arrival.

SriJoydip

Statutory Warning / Legal Disclaimer

This book, “Kalki The Arrival” is a work of fiction and creative imagination inspired by ancient narratives from the Mahabharata.

All characters, dialogues, locations, and sequences of events presented herein are products of the author’s imagination. Any resemblance—direct or indirect—to real persons, living or dead, or to actual institutions, organizations, or social groups is purely coincidental.

SriJoydip

While certain ideas, symbols, and philosophical elements from the Mahabharata have been reinterpreted in the context of modern society and politics, this work represents a contemporary retelling from an entirely new perspective.

The purpose of this work is not to offend or hurt the sentiments of any religion, community, historical, or mythological figure, but rather to inspire reflection on the modern relevance of ancient wisdom.

Readers/viewers are requested to engage with “Kalki Mahakak” purely as a literary and artistically constructed work of fiction.

Contents

SriJoydip

Chapter 1: What Was Taken, What Was Given

Suranjana

I knew before it happened.

Puri always speaks a second before it acts.

The crowd thickened near the Lion Gate. Incense, sweat, bells—everything louder than it needed to be. I felt the pull, gentle but firm, like a hand on the spine.

Do not resist.

That thought was not mine.

Two men passed me. No faces I could remember. No touch I could accuse. The ground dipped. Sound thinned. The temple vanished like a thought interrupted.

When my feet touched stone again, the air was cooler.

I was not afraid.

That surprised me.

"You are not taken," a voice said in the dark.

"You are relocated."

I laughed once. Short. Sharp.

"Why me?"

"Because fire remembers," the voice replied.

They did not bind me. They did not threaten me. They waited.

Time here did not move forward. It circled.

I understood then: this was not punishment.

It was custody.

Subimal

The chamber beneath the temple had no idols.

Only geometry.

Circles within squares. Lines that did not meet where the eye expected them to.

Chitrarath stood opposite me, his shadow refusing to behave.

"You asked for truth," he said.

"Not comfort."

I nodded.

He marked my forehead—not with ash, but with water.

Salted.

“Sight is not seeing,” he said.

“It is pattern recognition across lives.”

He placed his hand over my eyes.

Darkness arrived. Then pressure. Then release.

Images did not come.

Connections did.

Battles without blood. Decisions without endings. A wheel that fed on reaction. A boy who entered and never learned how to leave.

My breath broke.

“Chakṣuvidyā,” Chitrarath said.

“Not prophecy. Memory with discipline.”

I saw Suranjana—not as a woman, but as a principle.

Fire that witnesses. Fire that does not burn itself out.

“Where is she?” I asked.

“Where she must be,” he replied.

“So the cycle does not repeat.”

Suranjana

12 Kalki The Arrival.

SriJoydip

They did not interrogate me.

They listened.

When I spoke, the room changed shape. When I fell silent, it held.

“You carry the Draupadī principle,” the voice said.

“Not the story. The refusal.”

“I am not a character,” I said.

“Exactly.”

I slept without dreams.

When I woke, I was back in Puri—on a bench near the sea. Morning light. Vendors shouting. Life continuing, offended by nothing.

I checked my hands.

No marks.

Only certainty.

Subimal

When I came out of the chamber, the sea was calm.

Too calm.

Suranjana was sitting on a bench, feeding crumbs to birds.

Alive. Unharmed.

Unchanged.

Except for the way she looked at me—as if she had been waiting for me to catch up.

13 Kalki The Arrival.

SriJoydip

"You saw it," she said.

I nodded.

"And you?" I asked.

She smiled.

"I remembered."

That was when Chitrarath told us about Sambhala.

Not as refuge.

As delay.

Because the child would need time.

And the world—

would need distance.

Chapter Two : The Flight That Should Not Have Happened

The helicopter was not on any official route.

Its registration did not exist in public records.

Its fuel clearance had been denied twice.

And yet, it rose—cutting through cloud and silence—toward the upper Himalayas.

Inside sat three people.

Chitrarath, calm as ever.

Suranjana, quiet, alert.

15 Kalki The Arrival.

SriJoydip

Subimal Roy, gripping the seat—not from fear, but from memory.

This was not their first journey together.

Only the last before everything changed.

Puri: Where the Cycle Began

Years earlier, Subimal had gone to Puri alone.

Officially, to write a piece on coastal temple economies.

Unofficially, because something had been pulling him there since childhood.

On the night of the Nabakalebara rituals, he couldn't sleep.

The sea was restless.

And then—

a voice behind him.

"You are late."

The man introduced himself as Chitrarath.

No priest. No sadhu. No official.

Just a presence that did not ask permission to be trusted.

"You have been walking around the story," Chitrarath said,

"without realizing you are inside it."

That night, in a closed chamber beneath the temple, Subimal was taught
Chakṣuvidyā—not divine sight, but pattern sight.

To see repetition across centuries.

To recognize unfinished lives.

“You were not born new,” Chitrarath told him.

“You returned.”

Suranjana’s Disappearance

While Subimal tried to reject the revelation, Suranjana arrived in Puri.

She had felt him calling—though no call had been made.

On the third day, she vanished.

No witnesses.

No ransom.

No police report that made sense.

Subimal searched like a man chasing his own shadow.

The sea gave no answers.

Chitrarath appeared again.

“To find her,” he said,

“you must go where the war never ended.”

Dwarka: The Unfinished Revelation

Dwarka was quieter than Subimal expected.

Ruins half-swallowed by the sea.

Streets built over memory.

There, in a chamber beneath collapsed stone, Chitrarath finally spoke plainly.

17 Kalki The Arrival.

SriJoydip

“You were Arjuna,” he said.

Subimal laughed.

Then stopped.

Because the memories did not arrive as images—but as reflex.

The way his body reacted to certain names.

The way guilt arrived without cause.

“And Suranjana?” he asked.

Chitrarath did not answer immediately.

“She carries the principle,” he said at last.

“Not the person.”

“The Draupadī principle,” he continued.

“Witness. Fire. Refusal to break.”

Subimal understood then why she had been taken.

Not as a hostage—

but as a key.

She was returned days later.

Unharmed.

Silent.

She never asked where she had been.

She already knew.

18 Kalki The Arrival.

SriJoydip

Why Sambhala

“You cannot stay in the world now,” Chitrarath told them.

“Not with what is coming.”

Subimal resisted.

He still believed in journalism. In exposure. In reason.

Chitrarath shook his head.

“Kalki will not arrive where cameras are waiting.”

That was when Suranjana spoke for the first time since her return.

“The child will need silence,” she said.

“And time.”

The Helicopter

So the helicopter was arranged.

Unmarked. Untraceable.

As it lifted off from the coast, Subimal looked down at the sea swallowing Dwarka inch by inch.

“Is this how it ends?” he asked.

Chitrarath corrected him.

“This is how it pauses.”

Ahead, the mountains opened.

Sambhala waited.

And none of them said the name—

but all three knew:

The child would not belong to prophecy.

Prophecy would belong to him.

Closing Line

As the helicopter vanished into cloud,

the world below continued arguing—

unaware that the story it feared most

had already changed locations.

Chapter Three : Before the Child Was Born

No one in Śambhala trusted arrivals.

Especially not from the plains.

SriJoydip

So when Chitrath returned from Dwarka with two outsiders, the village noticed.

He did not announce them. He never did. But people saw the dust on his boots, the salt stains on his cloak, the way he walked faster than usual—as if time itself were chasing him uphill.

Behind him came a man and a woman.

The man looked tired. Not from travel—but from knowing too much. His eyes missed nothing and trusted even less. The woman walked slowly, one hand resting on her belly, her face calm in a way that unsettled people more than fear ever could.

"Who are they?" someone whispered.

"Why now?" another asked.

No one asked Chitrath directly.

Chitrath was not the kind of man you questioned.

Whispers Begin

That evening, the tea stalls stayed open longer.

"They say the woman is with child."

"They say the man is a seer who left the world."

"They say Dwarka sent them away."

"No," someone corrected, lowering his voice. "They were brought."

An old monk, bent with age, stared into his cup.

"There is a saying," he murmured, "that Śambhala does not receive guests. It receives answers."

21 Kalki The Arrival.

SriJoydip

The words spread.

By nightfall, speculation had outrun facts.

The Name No One Spoke

No one said the name.

But everyone thought it.

Kalki.

The last time that name had been spoken openly, a generation earlier, three houses had burned in a single night—no one knew how. Since then, prophecy was treated like fire: useful only at a distance.

“This is not the age for avatars,” a trader said.

“This is exactly the age for them,” someone replied.

Fear changed sides with every sentence.

Subimal’s Reputation Arrives First

By the second day, people knew who the man was.

Subimal Roy.

The journalist who had predicted wars before they happened. The man who had walked away from the world’s largest news empire. The one who vanished when his words became too accurate.

“If he is here,” someone said, “it is not by accident.”

“And if the woman carries his child?” another asked.

The question hung in the air, unanswered.

Suranjana did not address the whispers.

She walked slowly through the village, greeting children, touching stone walls, listening to the wind as if it spoke a language only she understood.

Some villagers felt calm near her.

Others felt watched.

A young girl asked her once, innocently, “Auntie, is your baby special?”

Suranjana smiled.

“Every child is,” she said.

That answer disturbed people more than any prophecy.

Chitrath’s Silence

Chitrath said nothing.

When asked why he had brought them here, he replied only once:

“Because the road ended.”

When asked how long they would stay, he said:

“As long as time allows.”

After that, no one asked again.

The Night Before

On the seventh night, the dogs began to behave strangely.

They did not bark.

23 Kalki The Arrival.

SriJoydip

They watched the mountains.

The river slowed.

An old bell rang by itself at the abandoned shrine near the ridge.

Someone swore the stars were shifting.

Someone else laughed too loudly and went home early.

Inside the stone house, Suranjana sat quietly.

Subimal paced.

“This was not how I imagined it,” he said.

Suranjana placed her hand on her belly.

“No one ever imagines the right age,” she replied.

Outside, Śambhala held its breath.

Because everyone felt it now—

Something was coming.

Not with weapons.

Not with fire.

But with consequences.

And before the child was born,

the world had already begun

to argue about him.

24 Kalki The Arrival.

SriJoydip

Chapter Four : The Night Kalki Was Born

No one in Śambhala knew that the night would be remembered.

The village slept early, as it always did. Nestled between black mountains and white peaks, Śambhala was used to silence. The wind spoke more often than people. Stars felt closer here. News from the world below arrived late—if at all.

That night, the dogs did not bark.

The river did not rush.

Even the prayer flags on the ridge hung still, as if listening.

Inside a small stone house, Suranjana lay awake.

Her time had come.

A Child the Mountains Waited For

Subimal stood outside, pacing. He had reported wars, collapses, revolutions. He had stared into the future and written it before it happened. Yet now, he was helpless.

Inside, Suranjana did not cry out.

She breathed.

Slow. Deep. Steady.

As if she had done this before.

Far above, clouds gathered—not storm clouds, but heavy, luminous ones, glowing faintly from within. Shepherds later swore the moon looked closer that night. One old monk claimed the stars had shifted.

When the child was born, there was no thunder.

Only silence.

And then—

a single cry.

Clear. Strong. Unafraid.

The midwife froze.

The baby opened his eyes.

The Mark

He did not scream again.

He looked around—as if recognizing the room.

There was no divine glow, no miracle flame. Just a child. Healthy. Calm.

But Subimal noticed something strange.

The baby's gaze did not wander.

It rested.

As if he was already listening.

"Gopal," Suranjana said softly.

The name felt right.

Outside, a sudden gust of wind rushed down the valley, setting the prayer flags into motion at once—red, blue, yellow, white, green—spinning like a wheel.

The moment passed.

27 Kalki The Arrival.

SriJoydip

The night returned to normal.

Or so it seemed.

Whispers in Śambhala

By morning, the village knew.

Not because anyone announced it—but because things felt different.

An old woman who had not slept without pain in years woke up rested. A broken bridge held firm though it should have collapsed. A child who could not speak laughed for the first time.

People did not call it a miracle.

They called it coincidence.

But they remembered the night.

Some said the boy was lucky.

Others said he was dangerous.

One monk said nothing—only bowed when he saw the child.

The Father's Fear

Subimal did not want prophecy.

He had seen what prophecy did to children.

He burned old notebooks. Locked away recordings. Refused visitors. When people asked questions, he answered with silence.

"This child will not be a symbol," he told Suranjana.

She only smiled.

"He will choose," she said.

At night, when Gopal slept between them, Subimal sometimes spoke—half awake, half dreaming.

Stories of ancient wars. Of wheels within wheels. Of battles that were lost not by force, but by confusion.

Suranjana listened.

So did the child.

A Quiet Beginning

Gopal grew like any other boy.

He fell. He laughed. He learned.

But there were signs.

He noticed patterns others missed. He grew quiet when arguments became loud. He asked questions no one could answer—and did not insist on answers.

When elders argued, he left.

When bullies shouted, he watched.

When storms came, he stood still.

People began to say, "He is different."

Others replied, "He is just observant."

Both were right.

The World Stirs

Far from Śambhala, the world began to shake.

29 Kalki The Arrival.

SriJoydip

Markets crashed. Beliefs hardened. Truth split into versions. Everyone spoke. No one listened.

Somewhere, old forces smiled.

Time was turning.

Not toward destruction—

but toward decision.

Closing

On his twelfth birthday, Gopal stood on the ridge above the village.

Below him lay Śambhala.

Beyond it—the world.

He did not know his destiny.

But destiny knew him.

The wheel had begun to turn.

And Kalki had already arrived—

not with fire,

not with a sword,

but with the quiet strength

to walk into chaos

and remember

how to come out.

Appendix

Kalki The Arrival is published by Sri Joydip Ashram Publications which conduct courses on some of the spiritual experience of Kalki Mahakal. Here is the Course path for experiencing that.

Sri Joydip Ashram Course Path – A Structured Approach to Yogic Learning and Healing

The Sri Joydip Ashram Learning Path: A Journey of Self-Realization, Healing, and Teaching

At **Sri Joydip Ashram**, yoga is not merely a practice—it is a **sacred journey of transformation**, guiding individuals toward **self-healing, expanded consciousness, and professional mastery**. Our structured course path offers a **progressive immersion** into the wisdom of **Surya Yoga and Gyan Yoga**, empowering students to evolve from seekers to **certified teachers of higher consciousness**.

1. Foundational Course: The Lifewise Program

◈ *Awakening Conscious Living Through Yoga*

The **Lifewise Program** is the **gateway to self-discovery** at Sri Joydip Ashram, designed for adult learners seeking to integrate yoga into their daily lives. Rooted in the **seven yoga habits**, this program nurtures **mental clarity, emotional resilience, and inner harmony.**

📍 **Structure:**

- **Duration:** 12 classes (24 hours) over one month
- **Investment:**
  - □12,000 (pay-per-class)
  - □10,000 (full advance payment, metropolitan cities)

📍 **Key Benefits:**

✓ Mastering **mindfulness and breathwork** to cultivate emotional balance
✓ Strengthening **mental resilience** against stress and anxiety
✓ Enhancing **energy alignment** for sustained well-being

Scientific research affirms that **regular yoga practice** fosters **neurological balance, stress reduction, and heightened cognitive function** (Khalsa et al., 2015; Field, 2011). Many students report profound shifts—**greater clarity, emotional stability, and an expanded sense of presence.**

2. Young Minds Program: Yoga for Youth Empowerment

◆ *Shaping Future Leaders with Clarity and Strength*

Designed for **students and young adults**, the **Young Minds Program** is a powerful tool for **intellectual and emotional empowerment**. It provides young learners with the **inner discipline** to navigate modern challenges while enhancing their **cognitive and emotional intelligence**.

📌 **Structure:**

- **15 Classes** tailored for youth development

📌 **Core Transformations:**

✓ **Increased concentration** and academic performance
✓ **Greater self-awareness** and emotional intelligence
✓ **Inner resilience** to face academic and social pressures

Research by **Harvard Medical School (2016)** highlights that yoga **boosts memory, attention, and cognitive function**, making it a **powerful accelerator of youth potential**.

3. Customizable Healing & Deep Practice Courses

◈ *Personalized Pathways for Self-Healing & Growth*

Upon completing foundational training, students can customize their practice, choosing specific **healing-oriented courses** based on their unique needs.

📌 Options:

✓ **12-class deep practice blocks** for progressive Surya Yoga mastery
✓ **Healing-focused courses** tailored for mental and physical well-being

A **Stanford University (2019) study** on sunlight exposure underscores the **scientific foundation** of **Surya Yoga's solar-based techniques**, showing their profound effects on **mood regulation, circadian rhythm balance, and energy restoration**.

---

4. Advanced Training: The Teacher's Path to Mastery

🔶 *Becoming a Torchbearer of Yoga Wisdom*

For those drawn to **share the light of yoga**, Sri Joydip Ashram offers **two levels of teacher certification**, designed to cultivate **profound wisdom, teaching expertise, and mastery of Surya Yoga**.

📌 **Lifewise Teachers Training Program (200 Hours)**

✔ **Duration:** 21 days

✔ **Investment:** □50,000

✔ **Core Training:**

- Deep immersion in **yoga philosophy & mindfulness practices**

- Mastery of **asana sequencing, breathwork, and teaching techniques**
- Development of **holistic teaching methodology**

❀ *Outcome:* Graduates emerge as **competent instructors**, capable of guiding students with an **integrated approach to yoga and self-transformation.**

📍 **2. Advanced Teachers Training Program (500 Hours)**

✔ **Duration:** 48 days

✔ **Investment:** □80,000

✔ **Advanced Training:**

- Profound Surya Yoga **energy mastery**
- Therapeutic applications for **mental and emotional healing**
- Teaching expertise aligned with **global certification standards**

❀ *Outcome:* This program prepares **world-class yoga educators** who can teach in **wellness centers, corporate programs, international retreats, and therapeutic settings.**

A Journey Beyond Teaching—A Path to Higher Consciousness

At **Sri Joydip Ashram**, yoga is not a mere discipline but a **way of being**—a journey into the depths of **self-awareness, energy alignment, and inner mastery**. Every course is meticulously structured to **awaken the seeker, empower the practitioner, and refine the teacher**, ensuring that each student experiences:

✨ **Physical rejuvenation through Surya Yoga's solar energy alignment**
✨ **Mental clarity and emotional balance through Gyan Yoga's wisdom practices**
✨ **Spiritual awakening through conscious living and self-realization**

By making **profound yoga education accessible and transformative**, Sri Joydip Ashram **empowers individuals** to lead **enlightened, purposeful, and balanced lives**—as both **practitioners of self-healing** and **teachers of higher consciousness.**

Are you ready to embark on this **sacred journey of transformation?**

37 Kalki The Arrival.

SriJoydip

Sri Joydip is a consciousness educator, author, filmmaker, and cultural practitioner working at the intersection of ethics, mental health, and lived spirituality.

With over two decades of experience, he is the founder of Sri Joydip Ashram Gyan Yoga Training & Research Centre and the creator of the Seven Yoga Habits and Lifewise frameworks—widely used for addressing anxiety, OCD, addiction, burnout, and moral fatigue through structured inner discipline rather than motivational rhetoric.

He is the author of multiple acclaimed books, including Seven Yoga habits That Can Transform Your Life, Arunachala Diaries: Living a Different Reality, Science of Yoga, Neem Baba, Lifewise: Yoga Recipe for Living Wisely, Living Wisely with Meditation,and Buddha: Art of Mindfulness.

His work is used as course material in institutional settings and has been internationally recognized for its depth and practicality.

A long-time participant in India's cultural ecosystem, his films have been screened at major festivals, including the Kolkata International Film Festival.

Sri Joydip's work emphasizes ethical wellness, cultural responsibility, and the recovery of wisdom in an age of distraction.

www.ingramcontent.com/pod-product-compliance
Lightning Source LLC
Chambersburg PA
CBHW062204160726
48282CB00027B/997